THE
TEAM
CURSE

LEAGUE OF THE PARANORMAL

THE TEAM CURSE

ISRAEL KEATS

DARBY CREEK
MINNEAPOLIS

Darby Creek
An imprint of Lerner Publishing Group, Inc.
241 First Avenue North
Minneapolis, MN 55401 USA

For reading levels and more information, look up this title at www.lernerbooks.com.

Image credits: Image Source/Getty Images (hands); msan10/Getty Images (player icon); LoudRedCreative/Getty Images (texture); komkrit Preechachanwate/Shutterstock.com (texture).

Main body text set in Janson Text LT Std
Typeface provided by Adobe Systems

Library of Congress Cataloging-in-Publication Data

Names: Keats, Israel, author.
Title: The team curse / by Israel Keats.
Description: Minneapolis : Darby Creek, [2019] | Series: League of the paranormal | Summary: "When Isaac joins the notoriously terrible Middleton High baseball team, he gets frustrated by the lack of effort from his teammates. But then he learns the team is cursed and becomes determined to end it"— Provided by publisher.
Identifiers: LCCN 2018051988 (print) | LCCN 2018056155 (ebook) | ISBN 9781541556997 (eb pdf) | ISBN 9781541556836 (lb : alk. paper) | ISBN 9781541572980 (pb : alk. paper)
Subjects: | CYAC: Baseball—Fiction. | Blessing and cursing—Fiction. | Supernatural—Fiction.
Classification: LCC PZ7.1.K396 (ebook) | LCC PZ7.1.K396 Te 2019 (print) | DDC [Fic]—dc23

LC record available at https://lccn.loc.gov/2018051988

Manufactured in the United States of America
1-46117-43492-4/10/2019

1

"Are you sure about this, Isaac?" Mr. Eglesby, the Middleton High Mustangs baseball coach, gave Isaac Little a hard look. He was talking to the players one by one after tryouts, telling them if they made the cut or not. Isaac had waited to go last, so nobody would see if he got cut.

He nodded. He wasn't completely sure, but he knew better than to say so.

"You told me you've never gone out for any sport," the coach said. "So why now?"

"I want to be on a team," Isaac said.

The coach's eyes narrowed. "Why not the chess club? Something like that might be more your speed."

"I want exercise," Isaac explained. *And I'm actually bad at chess*, he thought. People assumed that because he was small for his age and wore glasses, he was only interested in nerdy things.

"I want to be sure you're serious about this," the coach said.

"Of course I'm serious," Isaac said. During the tryouts, he had sprinted around the bases with the others, swung the bat, fielded grounders, and run after fly balls. He'd put in a lot of effort. That should have been enough to show he was serious.

The coach rubbed his jaw. He seemed to be thinking it over. "Do you know what our record was last year?"

Isaac shook his head. "No, but I know it wasn't very good."

"Zero and twenty," the coach said. "We didn't win one game. And none of those games were even *close*."

Isaac tried to look surprised and failed. The terribleness of the baseball team was well known around the school. It was well known around the entire city. Maybe even the entire state.

"The season before that wasn't as bad," the coach said.

"Oh?" Isaac said.

"We were only zero and nineteen," the coach explained. "One game was rained out and we never made it up."

Isaac snorted a nervous laugh.

"That's why I thought you might be doing this on a lark," the coach said. "Not many kids go out for the team unless they really love sports."

"I really do want to be on the team," Isaac told him.

"It's a big commitment," the coach told him. "Regular practices. Two or three games a week. And losing is hard on anyone." He shook his head. "It takes a lot out of you to lose the way we lose, game after game, year after year. But this is still a varsity team. I won't tolerate quitting or slacking off. You show up, you run the drills, you come to the games and give it your all."

"Yes, Coach. I understand."

"All right, then. You need to work on fundamentals, but you run the bases well."

"Really?"

"Really. You can switch into high speed better than most kids, and you turn a tight corner."

"Thanks." Isaac didn't know that about himself. It had probably come from his experiences fleeing from bullies back when he was in middle school. So far high school was better—he mostly walked through the halls without anybody noticing him.

"See you tomorrow at three o'clock sharp," the coach told him.

Isaac crossed the field. He felt like he was dreaming.

The truth was that being invisible wasn't that great. He wanted to be known for something. He was pretty good at school, but that didn't make him unique. And he wanted a group of buddies to hang out with. He mostly kept to himself during his freshman year because he'd been afraid of being bullied again, but now he felt ready to come out of his shell. He'd always envied sports teams, the way they seemed to hang together even off the field.

He'd never imagined he'd be on one himself, let alone at the varsity level. Even one with a terrible record.

***

"I went out for baseball," he told his parents that night.

"No kidding?" His dad's forkful of potatoes stopped halfway between the plate and his mouth. "Baseball, huh? Since when did you want to do that?"

"I've always liked baseball!" Isaac said.

"I know. We always have fun at the Millers games."

The Millers were a minor-league team. The Little family went to one or two games every summer.

"But you never mentioned playing before." Isaac's dad finally took his bite of food.

"Well, I'm proud of you for trying," his mother said, her voice full of pity.

"Mom, I made the team."

"Wow!" His mother tried to hide her surprise. "I mean, of course you did."

"He said I was fast on the bases."

"That's great!" They resumed eating for a few minutes, but Isaac noticed his father shooting him worried looks.

"So," his dad finally said. "The baseball team. When I was a student there, they weren't exactly good. In fact, they were famous for being bad. I don't think they won a game the whole time I was there."

"They're still bad," Isaac admitted. *And now they know why I made the team*, he thought.

"They are," his dad said. "Not that I exactly follow them, but word gets around."

"I bet," Isaac said.

"Are you braced for it, if you lose a lot?" his dad asked. "That's what I want to know. It can wear you out. Even professional athletes struggle with it."

"I'll be OK," Isaac said, hoping he was right.

2

It felt good to get dressed before the first practice. Isaac felt taller and tougher, knowing he was an actual athlete. A *varsity* athlete, no less. Most of the other kids on the team were bona fide jocks. Todd Blankenship, a senior, was the quarterback of the football team. Mike Wilson was a hockey goalie and captain. Jaxon Fields was on the swim team and played basketball.

Just hanging out with those guys will raise me up a rung or two, Isaac thought.

He wanted to chat with someone, but the other players barely spoke to each other. Just an occasional "Hi" or "Excuse me" as they put on their workout clothes and laced up their shoes. And nobody said a word to Isaac. It was as if they didn't even see him.

"I know we've had a rough couple of years," the coach said after they trooped outside for practice.

"Rough couple of centuries," one of the players said. His name was Korey. Isaac knew him a little bit because he was in the same homeroom. He was the only other new player on the team.

"Never mind all that," the coach said. "The slate is clean. Right now we're tied for first place in the conference with seven other teams. Zero wins and zero losses." The players nodded, but there wasn't a lot of hope or enthusiasm in their eyes.

They ran laps, then took turns swinging the bat and fielding grounders. The coach watched, taking notes.

"Most of you are coming back and can play the same positions as last year. But you—" he pointed at Isaac. "We need a center fielder."

Isaac jolted. "Isn't that position for a more experienced player?" he asked.

"You're a good runner. I bet you can cover a lot of ground," the coach said.

"But I, uh, I'm not that good at catching the ball."

"I'll teach you how to run down a ball and keep it in your glove," the coach assured him. Isaac felt a mixture of pride and fear. He'd been expecting to spend most of every game on the bench, but now he had a starting position. It was a big deal. But it also meant there were a lot of ways he could let the team down.

***

Over the next few days, Isaac learned where to stand based on the hitter, how to crouch and be ready to spring, and how to keep his eyes on the ball. He learned to run on his toes and keep his glove low so he didn't block his own line of sight. By the day before their first game, he was at least able to get under a fly ball, but time after time he missed the catch or watched the ball bounce out of his glove.

He walked back to the locker room feeling awful.

"You've made a lot of improvement in a short time," the coach told him.

"Thanks." Isaac still felt awful.

As he showered and dressed, none of the other guys talked to him. They spoke to each other in low whispers he couldn't hear. He pretended he didn't care, but tried to pick up at least a little of what they were saying. He did hear "West Side Park," and "tonight at midnight."

Were they having a get-together and not inviting him? He lingered in the locker room long after he was dressed. Somebody might see him and remember he hadn't been told about the get-together at West Side Park. But the Mustangs left, one by one, until the only two left were him and Todd.

"See you at the game tomorrow," the star quarterback said.

At least somebody was talking to him.

***

Isaac couldn't sleep. He was too worried about tomorrow's game, and too curious about the secret get-together at West Side Park. It was almost midnight. What kind of party did upperclassmen have on a weeknight at midnight? And at West Side Park of all places, which wasn't even anywhere near their neighborhood?

He finally got up and crept down to the garage. West Side Park was about three miles away, in a more run-down part of town, but a bike path went straight there. He got on his bicycle and pedaled madly. He would just see what they were up to, and then come back.

He was there in about fifteen minutes. He saw other bikes and a couple of cars in the parking lot. The sign said the park was officially open from 6 a.m. to 10 p.m., but he saw a group of people near the picnic area. He parked his bike and crept over. Sure enough, as he got closer he heard familiar voices. Todd, Jaxon, Mike. All of the other players. They were suited up and walking slowly toward the baseball field, carrying bats and gloves.

It's not a party, he realized. *It's a practice.*

He sprinted between the lampposts to stay in the darkness and got closer to the fence that ran along the third base line. The Mustangs had taken their fielding positions and now started to practice. The field lights were off, and he could only see them by the nearby street lamps.

Are things so desperate that we need a midnight practice? he thought.

He realized there was nobody in center field. *Why wouldn't they invite me? They need someone out there.*

He thought about running out on the field, but if he did they would know he'd been spying on them. He decided to just watch them for now.

But as the practice went on, Isaac noticed that there was something wrong. The players went through the motions slowly, as if they were puppets on strings. Their long shadows extended like skeletons across the grass towards him. The strangest thing was that there was nobody at the plate. No batter, yet the fielders played as if they had an opponent. The third baseman ran up the line, grabbed at the ground and hurled a throw toward first. The first baseman leaped to catch the throw, then shake his head as he missed and an invisible runner ran to second.

Isaac's heart began to race. *What is going on?* Whatever it was, he didn't want to stick around to find out. He raced back to his bicycle and sped home as if his teammates' shadows were still reaching for him.

3

The Mustangs' first game was at home against
the Emerson Eagles. Isaac suited up and felt
a jolt of pride wearing the Mustang colors of
mustard yellow and black trim. The other
players dressed slowly. Their eyes were rimmed
with dark rings. *No wonder*, Isaac thought. *They
were up in the middle of the night.* He'd been
thinking about the strange practice all day. But
he didn't know any of the other players well
enough to ask about it. Especially since they
hadn't invited him to whatever it was.

"Remember what I told you all," the coach
said in the dugout. "We have a clean slate.
Don't let last season drag you down."

"Yay," Korey said dryly. Isaac realized he hadn't seen Korey at the practice. Maybe he wasn't invited either? It made Isaac feel a little better about being left out. They were excluding both of the new kids.

Not that the night practice had done the other players any good. They scuffled out to their positions in the field, hanging their heads, looking like they might fall asleep on their feet.

Come on, guys, he thought. *We can at least try.*

The first pitch was hit deep to the outfield. Isaac sprang to his feet and went after it, running on his toes. He caught up to the ball and held his arm out, remembering to keep the glove from blocking his sight of the ball. The ball hit the webbing of his glove, but then suddenly bounced out, rolling to the wall. It was as if his glove was made of rubber.

"Ahh!" Isaac yelped. He ran after the ball, picked it up near the wall, and hurled it toward Todd, the shortstop. The runner was already on his way to third base. Isaac glanced at the official scoreboard and saw the numeral "1" appear by the big "E" for the home team. Great. He had already made an error. The first error of the season. They were off to a rotten start because of him.

Two runners scored before they got out of the inning.

"Don't worry about dropping that ball," Korey told him, giving him a nudge. "We'll lose anyway."

Isaac smiled weakly.

"It's all right," the coach said, clapping his hands. "We have the rest of the game to make that up. Let's hit now! Don't give them any easy outs."

Mike was the leadoff hitter. He took a feeble swing at the first pitch and missed, hit the second one foul, and struck out on the third. The next two batters didn't do any better.

"Come on, come on. I said no easy outs!" Mr. Eglesby was starting to sound mad.

"You guys are pathetic!" A voice rang out over the dugout as Isaac ran back to center field. He looked over his shoulder and saw an old man glaring from the bleachers.

"Never mind him," Jaxon, the left fielder, told him. "He comes to every home game."

"What, is his grandson on the team?" Isaac asked.

"Would he heckle like that if he did?" Jaxon asked, one eyebrow raised.

"Ha, probably not," Isaac admitted. "But why else would he come to every game?"

"Maybe he's got nothin' better to do," said Jaxon. "Or maybe he likes heckling."

Well, he sure picked the right team, Isaac thought.

He took his position in center. He remembered to shade himself in the direction of the batter's hit and keep his eyes on the ball. This time, his hard work at practice paid off. The batter hit a fly ball straight toward him, and he actually made the catch. He lobbed the ball to the shortstop, hoping to stop a runner on third base from scoring, but Todd threw the ball lazily to the catcher, Mike, missing by a few feet and a few seconds.

I know you can throw better than that, Isaac thought, shocked. *I've seen you hit a receiver's hands from that same distance during a football game, and now there aren't guys trying to tackle you.*

Later that inning, a throw to the plate rolled through the catcher's legs. Another runner crossed the plate.

A high-speed hockey puck can't get by you, Mike, but a slow-rolling baseball can? Isaac thought.

The game dragged on. The Eagles added two or three runs per inning, while the Mustangs could barely get a runner on base. Mr. Eglesby shook his head and sighed as he filled in the scorecard.

Their first chance came when Todd hit a single. There were two outs, but at least they had a base runner. It was Isaac's turn to bat.

Don't blow it. Don't blow it. Don't blow it, he told himself. He got good metal on the ball and bounced it through the infield. He charged to first, hoping Todd could make it to second. But Todd ran slowly, like he knew he didn't have a chance, and was out at second.

"Tough luck," Isaac told Todd as they trotted back to the dugout to get their gloves.

"Whatever," Todd said tiredly.

As he went to center, Isaac thought about that play. Todd should have been running from the moment Isaac swung the bat. Todd could have taken the base if he'd been paying attention. It could have been a base hit instead of an out.

He doesn't care, Isaac realized, his heart sinking. *None of these guys care.*

***

After five innings, the umpire called the mercy rule. The Mustangs were down by ten runs and hadn't gotten a player past first base.

"Welcome to Mustangs baseball," said Todd as they changed into their street clothes.

"Thanks," Isaac said. "I kind of think—" He wondered if it would be all right to say what was on his mind. Todd looked at him, both eyebrows up.

"Kind of think . . . ?"

"I kind of think we might have . . . I might have had a hit, and we might have scored a run . . . if you'd run on contact when I batted."

There was a moment of silence as the upperclassmen stared at him.

"Says the guy who's oh-for-one with an error," Mike finally said.

"But I played really hard," Isaac whispered.

"What are you saying? That none of us are trying?" Jaxon asked.

"No," Isaac said. It was exactly what he was *thinking*, but he hadn't actually *said* it.

The boys finished getting dressed in silence, keeping their backs turned to Isaac. One by one they left the locker room, some giving Isaac a hard look or snorting as they passed.

So much for making friends with people on the team.

As the players filed out, Todd stopped for a moment.

"Sorry I didn't run out that play," he said, placing a hand on Isaac's shoulder. "I was off my game there."

"Oh, um, it's OK," said Isaac. His voice sounded higher than usual, like a little kid. He wondered if that was how Todd saw him. Not as a teammate, but a little kid on a team for big kids. Someone to talk down to.

"Look," Todd said in a low voice, like he was sharing a secret. "We're a terrible team. Accept it. There are worse things than losing."

"Accept it?" *Is this really the same guy who once won a football game after being down 21–0?*

"It's just how it is. You'll learn it the hard way if you don't learn it the easy way." Todd shouldered his bag and left Isaac alone in the locker room.

I don't have to do this, Isaac thought, slamming his own locker shut and fighting down tears. *I said I wouldn't quit, but I could do it anyway. No reason to stick with a team that doesn't care and doesn't like me.*

He left, thinking he would walk to the coach's office and tell him he was quitting. He could make up an excuse. He'd say he had to babysit his little brother after school and couldn't make practices anymore. He didn't

have a little brother, but the coach didn't
know that.

But somehow his legs wouldn't walk that
way. He stood frozen in place for a long time,
unable to move. He tried lifting one foot, then
the other, but it was as if his legs had turned to
solid stone.

Maybe I don't want to quit, he finally thought,
and then his feet released their grip from the
floor. He turned and headed home.

4

The next Sunday night, he stared at the patches of moonlight on the ceiling and thought about the Mustangs. He knew by the red glowing numbers on his alarm clock that it was 11:30 p.m. Which meant he'd been lying awake for almost an hour. He'd gone to bed early to get a good night's sleep before the next day's game, but the sleep wasn't happening.

He heard his parents getting ready for bed. Water in the sink, footsteps in the hall. His door cracked for a moment.

"Sleep well, bud," his dad's voice said. "We're proud of you for sticking with this."

The door shut, and then the line of light under the door disappeared with a click.

Isaac punched his pillow and tried to get comfortable.

The truth was he didn't want to stick with it. He wanted to quit. But every time he had tried to walk to the coach's office after practice the past week, it was as if the air around him got thick and sticky. He couldn't move through it. When he did see the coach, he couldn't talk. His mouth was glued shut.

The clock ticked on to 11:40 p.m. He listened to outside noises—wind in the branches, an occasional distant dog barking.

I wonder if the team is having another night practice. If so, they didn't invite me again.

He got out of bed, got dressed, and started downstairs. His foot creaked on the step that always creaked.

"What's wrong, honey?" his mother's voice echoed down the hallway.

"I'm a little wound up about tomorrow's game. I'm going for a walk."

"At this hour?"

"Just around the block. I'll be fine, Mom."

He heard her mutter but she went back into the bedroom. He sighed with relief and made his way downstairs, got his bike from the garage, and pedaled to West Side Park.

Sure enough, the rest of the team was gathered in the practice field. This time, they were already playing, if you could call it that. More like going through a slow-motion replay of a game. He noticed that they still didn't have a ball. The pitcher would go into the windup and fling *nothing*, and the batter would swing at it. The fielders would chase *nothing* as the player ran to first base. Had they had a baseball last time? He'd been too far away to tell.

"Hey!" a hushed voice spoke behind him. He wheeled around and saw Korey looking at him with wide, disbelieving eyes.

"You know about this too?" he whispered.

Isaac nodded.

"What's going on? What are they doing?"

"Practicing," Isaac said, but his voice cracked. It was obvious that this was too strange to be a regular practice.

He glanced back at the team and saw that everyone was looking at him and Korey. It was no use trying to sneak away. They were caught.

One of the players waved them over.

They walked toward the diamond.

5

"Told you," said Todd to the other players as Isaac and Korey reached the infield. The outfielders had closed in, forming a loose circle around them. "The others thought you two might not come until midseason. Especially you." He tapped Isaac on the shoulder. "But I had a hunch you'd show up tonight."

"What's going on?" Korey asked.

"Now that you're all the way in, we can tell you," said Jaxon. "Come on." He led them toward the dugout. Isaac exchanged an uneasy look with Korey. This was getting weirder and weirder.

"All the way into *what?*" Korey mouthed.

Isaac shook his head. He didn't know either.

When they were in the dugout, Jaxon sat down on the bench and stifled a yawn. The rest of the team resumed their strange drill.

"So what's going on?" Korey asked, his voice loud and a little angry. His eyes were round, his teeth clenched. "What is this, some dumb prank?"

"I said the exact same thing three years ago," said Jaxon. "I found out about night practice and spied on it. When I saw the rest of the team going through this weird ritual, I was sure it was an elaborate joke making fun of the newbies. I ran out yelling that I was going to tell the coach. Well, it turned out it was deeper and darker than that."

"Deeper and darker how?" Isaac asked. He wasn't angry anymore. Just confused, and a little bit scared.

"That's what I'm trying to tell you," said Jaxon.

"Then tell us," Korey said. "Out with it."

"The Middleton High Mustangs baseball team is cursed," Jaxon said in a deep whisper.

Korey and Isaac traded looks again.

"Cursed how?" Korey asked, folding his arms. He still looked suspicious.

"How? We're forced to come here every night before a game. We fight it. We try to lock ourselves in our bedrooms, let the air out of our bike tires, whatever we can do to stop ourselves. But as midnight approaches, we get the urge to come down here." He waved his hand at the players on the field. "If you lock the door, you'll climb out a window. If you've let the air out of your tires, you'll walk. We've played in pouring rain and we've played with tornado sirens going off. One year there was a cold snap, but we were here, freezing to death. We've had guys show up sick and guys show up with broken arms. One year, a guy came when he'd had an appendectomy that very morning. He tore open his stitches."

Isaac cringed, almost feeling the pangs in his own stomach.

"I don't buy it," Korey said.

"Then leave," Jaxon said. "Right now. See you at the game tomorrow."

Korey glared at the dugout fence. He clenched his fists.

"You're not leaving," Jaxon taunted.

"This is stupid," Korey fumed.

"I know you *want* to leave. But I also know you can't get your body to stand up and walk out. And you." He nodded at Isaac. "I'll bet you tried quitting the team by now. But you couldn't do it, right?"

Isaac looked at the concrete dugout floor.

"It's happened to every one of us," Jaxon said. "We can't quit the team, we can't stop the night games. And we can't play well. Come on, you saw that. We're tired from being up all night, but there's more to it than that. When we run the bases, it feels like the infield has turned to quicksand. When we swing the bat, it seems to weigh a hundred pounds. When we catch a ball, it's like our glove can't close around it. The ball bounces out."

Isaac gulped. That had happened to him—only once so far, but it had resulted in that error.

"Does Mr. E know?" Korey asked.

"He knows something is up, but not what it is," Jaxon said. "We can't tell him. We can't talk about it to anyone except each other. If you're like me, you'll try. Your parents will beg you to tell them what's wrong, but all you can do is say 'Nothing' and mope. They'll write it off as you being a moody teenager. Or maybe they'll take you to see a therapist. Soon enough, the season is over, and you kind of forget in between seasons. Life will go back to normal until baseball starts up again."

"So what do we do?" Korey asked.

"Stick it out," Jaxon said. "Eventually you graduate and get out. The curse doesn't kill you. It just ruins your spring for four straight years. I knew this one guy, Stephen, who was a senior when I was a freshman. I've seen him since he graduated. He's doing all right. He's playing baseball for his college team. He's happy. He barely remembers playing for the Mustangs. I mentioned it and he laughed about how bad we'd been, and that was that. I don't think he remembers the curse. It's like a bad dream he had and forgot about.

"This is my last year. Soon it'll all be over. It's harder for you guys. You're just starting out." He got a sad look on his face. "But we do need you. It's been hard to get people to sign up. The team is so bad, it's a miracle anybody does. Only you two did this year. But I kind of have a feeling if we didn't find replacements, if we couldn't field a team, something bad would happen." He stood up. "We'd better get started." He walked slowly out onto the field. Isaac felt a tug on his arm, like someone was pulling him to follow Jaxon. He stood up and walked out to center field, unable to free himself from the strange tugging force. Out of the corner of his eye, he sensed people in the stands, but when he looked directly at them, there was nothing but shadows.

And now he saw a batter, sort of—the pale figure seemed to flicker in and out, and Isaac could see right through him to the backstop. The batter tapped the plate with a wooden bat and took a warm-up swing. That was almost as strange as everything else going on. Youth teams hadn't used wooden bats in a long time.

They always used aluminum, because metal wouldn't break and splinter.

The pitcher went into the stretch. Isaac saw now that there *was* a ball—a small gray sphere that flew from the pitcher's hand. The batter swung and the ball flew his way. He ran after it, glove outstretched—still led by forces beyond his control. The ball seemed to go through his glove and rolled away. As he chased it, Isaac realized the ball was both there and not there, like an optical illusion. He picked it up and felt nothing in his hand. The ball had no weight. Yet he could see gray stitches on the gray leather. It wasn't a baseball—it was the ghost of a baseball.

The ghostly batter circled first.

Isaac's arm flung it toward second. The ball skewed wide, missing by a mile.

The wind swirled around his head and seemed to be mocking him. There were no words, but it sounded human and taunting.

6

He woke up late the next morning. The night
before felt like a bad dream, but he knew it
wasn't. For one thing, he was dead tired. For
another, he was still dressed. All he'd done is
kick off his shoes and collapse onto the bed.
He couldn't remember what happened after he
threw that first pitch. It was as if the night game
had been wiped from his memory. He wasn't
even sure what time he'd gotten home, exactly,
but it must have been between 2 and 3 a.m.

He would give anything to take a sick
day, to skip school and miss the game. But
somehow he got up, stuffed his uniform into
his gym bag, and walked out of the house

without breakfast. The sunlight seemed harsh, and the birds especially loud.

I just have to make it through the day, he thought. *Then I can sleep.*

Isaac stumbled through his classes like a zombie. There was a test in algebra. The questions barely made sense, but he worked through them.

Half an hour before school got out, he waved his pass and was able to leave study hall. He'd been looking forward to that moment: the jealous looks of other students as he walked out of school early. But now he was too tired to enjoy it.

How am I going to get through a whole game? he wondered. *Or even half a game, if the umpires call the mercy rule again?*

The bus was already full when he climbed on. He plopped down in the first open seat. He realized he was sitting next to Mike.

"Welcome aboard," the catcher said. It seemed that he wasn't just welcoming Isaac to the bus. He was welcoming him to full-blown membership of the Mustangs, curse and all.

All I can do is try, he thought as they took the field. At first he did. He made one good running catch that got a smattering of applause from the stands. But in the third inning, he missed a ball by ten feet. It seemed like the ball was going to land right in his glove, but it sailed by, as if picked up by a sudden wind. The curse's doing.

He had two plate appearances. He tried to remember everything the coach had taught him. He took the right stance, batted with his whole body, and tried to drive the ball downfield. He felt like his swing was good when he was taking practice swings on deck, but the moment he went to the plate he started flailing. His brain told him to be patient, but his arms would swing early. His brain would tell him to follow through, but his hands would swat at the ball like it was a housefly. He struck out the first time, but surprised himself by hitting into a double play the second time.

I don't know if that's the curse or I'm just bad, he thought. It was hard to separate the two.

"Don't worry," the coach told him in the dugout. "Normal to have jitters your first few times out. You have good form. You'll get better."

Isaac wondered how many new players the coach had given little pep talks like this one. Did the coach ever wonder why so many players never did get better?

The Mustangs managed to avoid the mercy rule this time, and lost by *only* eight runs. Isaac sat next to Todd on the ride home, who was falling asleep. He nudged the shortstop with his elbow to wake him.

"What?"

"How long has it been going on?" Isaac whispered. Todd didn't have to ask him what he meant by *it*.

"I don't know. A long time." Todd shut his eyes again.

"We should figure out how long," Isaac said.

"Yeah, we should," Todd murmured.

"If we traced it back, maybe we could find out why we have the curse," Isaac said. "And if we figure *that* out, maybe we can break it."

"Sure we can. Can I go to sleep now?"

Isaac wanted to talk more, but Todd had already started snoring.

***

Isaac slept hard for ten hours and woke up feeling almost normal. But the curse weighed on his mind. The thought of eighteen more sleepless nights and hopeless games filled him with dread. And that was just this season. There would be two more seasons after this one, his junior and senior years. He'd never be able to do it.

Todd found him at lunch, set his tray across from his, and sat down. Isaac realized others were glancing at them, probably shocked that the popular quarterback was eating with a nerdy sophomore.

"Hey, remember what you said on the bus?" Todd whispered.

"Um . . ." Isaac tried to remember.

"About solving a problem," Todd said.

"Oh, yeah. Of course." *Breaking the curse.* Isaac tried to say that out loud, but his voice failed in his throat.

"I think you're right. We should do that."
Todd picked up a carrot and crunched into it.
"I've tried to talk the other guys into it, but
they say there's no point. They're too tired to
fight this thing. But I think we should try."

"But what do we do?" Isaac asked.

"First, we need to figure out when this
whole thing started." Todd dropped his voice
even lower, and shielded his mouth with his
hand, "If we find the last time the Mustangs
won, and the beginning of the losing streak,
the answer will be in between."

"That's a great idea," Isaac said.

"But I don't know how," Todd admitted.
"It's not like we can ask around."

"What about the school newspaper?" Isaac
suggested. "They have the archives at the media
center. We could ask Ms. Wesley if we can see
them." Ms. Wesley was the school librarian.
She'd been there for years. Probably decades. "I
have study hall in the library last period. I could
ask her."

"If you can," said Todd. Isaac knew what
he was thinking—the curse could turn

their legs to cement as they walked into the library, or seal their mouths as they went to the librarian.

"Worth a try," said Isaac. "Maybe it'll work if we go at it in a roundabout way."

"I'll come with you," Todd said. "I have class, but I can wiggle out of it." He wolfed down half his sandwich in a few bites. "Being a star athlete has its privileges."

***

The library was always busy during last period, with a dozens of students studying, chatting, and trying to sneak some social media time on the computers. Isaac waited, backpack slung across his shoulder, wondering if Todd would show up. Ten minutes into the period, he finally did.

"Told my biology teacher I was feeling sick," he said. "It wasn't even a lie. We were dissecting frogs." He thumped Isaac on the shoulder. "Come on, let's do it." As they walked to the library desk, Isaac again felt like people were watching them.

Ms. Wesley seemed surprised they were together too. She stood up as they approached the library desk.

"Well, hello, Todd. And Isaac. Can I help you with something?"

"Do you have back issues of the school newspaper?" Todd asked.

"Oh, we have the complete run," she said. "All the way back to when the school opened over eighty years ago."

"Awesome," said Todd.

"What are you researching?" she asked.

Isaac's mouth felt gummed shut, and he knew he couldn't tell her about the curse, or even that they were looking into the history of the baseball team. He saw the same strained look on Todd's face.

"Just, uh, school history," Isaac finally blurted out. He could speak just fine as long as he didn't try to talk about the curse or the baseball team.

"Well, we only have the last ten years up here," she said. "If it's older than that, we'd need to go to the storage room."

"It is definitely older than that," Isaac told her. "Where's the storage room?"

"In the basement, but I can't leave my desk." She took a key hanging near the desk and handed it to Isaac. It was big and tarnished with a bit of rust. She lowered her voice. "Through the office, out the back door, and down the steps. I trust you, but don't make me regret it!"

"I can't believe she's letting us do this," Todd said as they slipped through the office.

"Being a nerd also has its privileges," Isaac replied.

But he was surprised their feet didn't turn to cement, that the door in the back wasn't sealed shut. Was the curse really going to let them do this? The door led to a steep, narrow flight of stairs. At the bottom was a heavy metal door. Todd turned the key in the lock. The door swung open with a deep creaking sound. They entered a cold, dark room lined with metal shelves and cabinets. It smelled damp and musty. Todd fumbled at the wall and found a switch, turning on a single bare bulb that barely cut through the darkness. Isaac squinted at labels on the cabinets.

Middleton Student News, each cabinet said, followed by a range of years.

"This is it," he said. He traced the decades down to the bottom and opened the drawer labeled "1980." For a split second he stared into what looked like a drawer full of shimmering black jelly. He gulped.

"What?" Todd said.

The jelly erupted and spilled out on the floor, spreading and slithering away. Not jelly, but a swarm of inky-black bugs. Isaac had never seen so many bugs at once.

"Ack!" Todd yelped and ran for the door. Isaac followed, slamming and locking the door while Todd pounded up the stairs. Isaac found him on the stop step, doubled over and heaving.

"Hate. Bugs. Worse than. Frogs!" he said between breaths. His voice cracked. He wasn't quite sobbing, but he was close. Isaac could only nod. The shock of seeing Todd shaking like a scared child was even worse than the bugs.

"It's all right," Isaac said. "They're just silverfish. They don't bite people. They eat paper."

"Paper," Todd echoed, catching his breath. "And any facts we might have dug up."

"Yeah," Isaac agreed. He'd been too freaked by the sight of the bugs and Todd's meltdown to think about it what it meant. The newspapers were gone, and any chance they had to learn from them.

"That's bad luck," said Todd.

"I don't think it's luck," said Isaac. "I think the curse sent them."

7

"I know you can play better than you've been playing," the coach lectured at the end of practice that day. "I still believe that we can turn this season around."

Isaac tried to listen but found his mind wandering, picturing the stomach-turning sight of inky bugs pouring out of a metal drawer. *If the curse can send armies of insects to eat up the past, it's more powerful than us,* he thought.

"*Isaac!*" the coach barked. "Please pay attention."

"Huh? Sorry, Coach."

The coach resumed his speech. Isaac knew Mr. Eglesby didn't know about the curse. He probably wondered why the team was always so bad. Isaac remembered the way the coach had shaken his head over the scorecard during the first game.

The memory jolted him. *What does Coach do with the scorecard after each game?* he wondered. *Does he store them in folders and stuff them into a cabinet, season after season? And if so, did the silverfish get to them?* The gymnasium was a stand-alone building separate from the rest of the school. The curse would never let him ask the coach directly to see the old scorecards. But if he could somehow get a chance to go through the files, he might uncover some of the secret.

"So let's go into tomorrow's game with a whole different mindset," the coach finished. "Hit the showers." The players trooped to the locker room with heads hung, knowing that no matter what mindset they had, the game would be a disaster. Isaac saw the coach heading for the office.

"Hey, Todd." Isaac nudged him.

"Yeah?" Todd turned back.

"I need you to get the coach to run to the locker room. *After* he's unlocked the office."

"What are you talking about?"

"I'll explain later. But it has to do with our, uh, project."

Todd smiled.

As soon as the two of them entered the locker room, Todd pretended to slip on the wet floor. He fell backward and landed hard. The other players jumped.

"Ow! My back!" Todd wailed. The other players watched, confused. Isaac realized it was his turn to do something.

"Nobody move him," he said. "I'll get Coach!" He ran through the gym, down the stairs, and into the office. Mr. Eglesby looked up in surprise at Isaac.

"Todd is hurt!" Isaac panted.

"What? How?"

"He slipped in the locker room. He said it's his back."

"I'd better take a look. Nobody's tried to move him, right?"

"No, but you'd better go quick."

The coach grabbed his phone and a first aid kit and fled past Isaac, leaving the office door open. Isaac watched him disappear into the locker room, and then quickly turned to the filing cabinet. It was locked, but the coach's keys were on the desk. He undid the lock at the top of the cabinet, and scanned the labels on the drawers. They were organized by decade, the earliest one from the 1950s. That was so long ago Isaac could barely imagine it.

He opened it and fingered past folders for football, basketball, hockey, and wrestling. The earliest folder for baseball was 1958. Whoever coached the team before then must not have kept records. Isaac flipped through the scorecards in the folder and saw nothing but losing scores for the Mustangs. This meant they'd been on a losing streak for over sixty years. *The curse can't be* that *old, can it?*

He heard footsteps and quickly slid the door shut, locked the cabinet, and placed the keys back where he found them. As the coach walked in, he realized he still had the folder from 1958. He hid it behind his back.

"Todd says he took a spill and landed funny," Mr. Eglesby said. There was a little suspicion in his voice, but he probably couldn't imagine why Todd would lie about getting hurt. "He says he's all right now."

"Oh, good," said Isaac.

"I encouraged him to go have it checked. It would be a shame if he lost out on a football scholarship because he got hurt at a baseball practice." The coach nodded at the door. "See you tomorrow, Isaac."

"Yes, Coach." Isaac slipped past, hiding the folder on the opposite side of his body so the coach didn't notice. When he got back to the locker room, most of the players had left, but Todd was still there, sitting on the bench and wearing a black strap around his midsection.

"It's a back brace," Todd explained. "Coach made me wear it. He wants me to go to the hospital and have it looked at."

"You did too good an acting job. Maybe you should go out for drama club."

"Yeah, right. What if they have a curse, too?" Todd snorted.

Isaac laughed. "Anyway, I went through the filing cabinet in the coaches' office. The files go back sixty years, and we were cursed even then." He held up the folder.

"Wow. I didn't know it went back that far."

"Me neither. Our grandfathers could have been going those same creepy night games in West Side Park."

"It probably wasn't even a park then," Todd said. "They were probably standing in a cow pasture or something."

"Hope I can put this back before anyone notices it's gone." Isaac stuffed the folder into his backpack. "I'd better go home and nap before tonight's . . . you know."

"I know," Todd said. "Good idea. Me too."

"Don't forget that ER visit," Isaac said.

***

Isaac woke up early the next morning, fully dressed and completely drained. He could barely remember going to West Side Park, but he knew he'd been there. He had chased that ghost of baseball across the outfield while the wind howled and the shadows watched.

He plodded through the day, counting down the hours until he could sleep.

His last period was study hall. He went to the library to read a book for English class but couldn't concentrate. Ms. Wesley saw him and walked over.

"Hey," he greeted her. "Sorry again about those silverfish."

"Sorry for what?" she said. "It's not your fault we have an infestation! I'm sorry you and Todd had to discover them."

You don't know the truth of it, he thought. *We brought the curse into your library.*

"I was thinking," she said. "I know someone who might be able to help you with your research."

"Really?"

"Yes. His name is Bert Hawes. He used to be a teacher, and he ran the school newspaper for some time. He retired twenty years ago, but he still lives in town. A few blocks from the school, in fact. I drop by sometimes for tea." She quickly jotted something down on a piece of paper and handed it to Isaac. "Maybe you can ask him? He knows more about the history of this school than anyone."

"Thanks." Isaac looked at the paper. *Maple and 14th. Yellow house with black trim*, it read.

"I think I know the house," said Isaac. "It's Middleton colors?"

"Yep. He sure has school spirit," Ms. Wesley said. "I think he even used to coach the baseball team."

Isaac's heart skipped a beat. "Great. I'll talk to him." He pushed the paper into the pocket, wishing he could go straight after school. Unfortunately, the Mustangs had a game to play.

***

"Pathetic! Totally pathetic!" The old heckler was back, sitting behind the home dugout. The Mustangs were already down by six runs after three innings. It wasn't clear to Isaac if the guy was mad at the Mustangs for losing, or gloating.

Either way, he needs a better hobby, he thought.

"I'm so sick of that guy," Korey grumbled.

"You'll get used to him," Mike said. "I think he comes with the curse," he added in a whisper. A few of the players chuckled.

"I'm glad you find this funny!" the coach complained.

"Sorry, Coach," the players all said quickly. But after Mr. E turned back around, Todd elbowed Isaac and they grinned at each other.

I'm actually part of the team, Isaac thought. It did feel good, but still he wondered what it would feel like if they won a game.

8

"Do you want to go see this guy, Bert Hawes?" Isaac asked Todd the next day at lunch.

"Who's that?" Todd asked between bites of chicken sandwich.

"An old teacher. Ms. Wesley said he used to coach the baseball team. He might remember when the team started to lose."

"*If* we can ask him. And *if* he can remember."

"Well, it's our only lead," Isaac said. "You in?"

"Sure. Nothing better to do." Todd stifled a yawn. "Except sleep."

They met in the parking lot after school. Isaac had unlocked his bike. They headed toward the address that Ms. Wesley had given them.

"Looks like our school colors," Todd said as they approached the house.

"I know. He's a big Mustangs fan."

"Wait." Todd reached into his bag and removed the baseball cap, then pulled it down over his head. "You put on yours."

"How come?"

"Because the curse won't let us bring up baseball, but *he* might if he sees us in these."

"Good thinking." Isaac pulled out his own cap.

They rang the bell. A moment later the door opened a crack and a man peeked out. He had only a few wispy hairs and wire-rimmed glasses.

"What can I do for you boys?" he said. "Hey, do you go to MHS?" He pointed at their caps.

"We sure do," Isaac said.

"I used to teach there," he said. "A long time ago. You must be on the baseball team?"

"Yep," Isaac nodded. "Center field."

"Shortstop," Todd added.

Mr. Hawes threw the door open all the way. "Come in, come in. Mustangs baseball players are always welcome here." He led them down the hall to the living room. "Tell me, has the team gotten any better? I coached that cursed team for twenty years!"

Isaac felt a rush of adrenaline when Mr. Hawes said *cursed*.

"The Mustangs never could get anything good going, and had the worst luck," he went on. "We had good players, that's for sure. Boys who exceled at other sports. Even boys who exceled at baseball, when they weren't playing for the Mustangs. Why, one boy, Timothy Crayton, he went pro as a pitcher in '99!"

"Yeah, I know," Todd said. "His picture is on the wall of fame." The wall of fame was a display right inside of the school, featuring notable graduates from Middleton High. Business people, local officials, authors, and athletes. Isaac had looked over that wall a hundred times, wondering if his own name would end up there one day and what he would have done to earn it.

Mr. Hawes was still rambling about the losing streak.

"I used to blame myself, but no coach since has done any better, nor did the coaches before me. Anyway, what brings you here?"

"Oh, uh . . ." Isaac wanted to say *the curse*, but his mouth wouldn't let him.

"We're doing a history project," Todd managed to croak out. "About the Mustangs."

"Hm. Well, I don't know where to begin. I was mostly an English teacher, you know, but I played baseball in college, and once the principal found out, he tapped me to coach. I said I didn't know anything about coaching. He said, 'Bert, you'll be fine.' Well, I proved him wrong!" He laughed.

And he talked some more. And some more. Isaac and Todd couldn't steer him in the right direction, but Mr. Hawes liked to talk, and he liked to talk about the baseball team, so they hoped eventually he would get to the reason for the losing streak. And whether he really believed in a curse, or only used that word to mean a run of bad luck.

At last Mr. Hawes turned to the baseball team's history.

"Mind you, they were bad when I took the reins from . . . I forget his name. Larson or Olson, something like that—back in the 80s. Well, before *he* was coach, I think the team had some good years. Some great ones, even. But then *it* happened."

"Wha . . . ?" Isaac managed to start before his mouth clamped shut. This was it!

Todd leaned in, his eyes wide.

"Well, this is nothing but a rumor," Mr. Hawes said. "But the story goes that the Middleton Mustangs were once the best team in the county. But then they played this game against some small-town school with barely enough kids to field a team. And apparently the game was ugly. The Mustangs batted through the lineup a couple of times in just the first inning. The score was something crazy. Twenty-five to nothing. They didn't have the mercy rule back then, but the umpires said if the coaches agreed, they could just call it a game. But, well, the other coach was stubborn. 'Not until we have our chance to bat,' he said. And the Mustangs coach said, 'You have to get through the top of the inning first, don't you?'

"So the game dragged on and on, without even an out. Worse was that the other team had used up all their pitchers.

"Except one kid. He was small and scrawny and pale. He looked as if he was ten years old. Story has it that he'd just recovered from mono or scarlet fever or some such illness, and was being raised by his grandma. And this grandma was rumored to be . . ." Mr. Hawes lowered his voice and spoke in a whisper. ". . . *a witch*!"

Todd looked grim. Isaac didn't believe in witches, but he also hadn't believed in curses until a few weeks ago.

"Now, she was at that game, and when that boy took the mound, she stood up in the bleachers. It was like she was trying to stare down the Mustangs. 'Go easy on him,' she seemed to say. 'Make three outs so we can call the game and go home.'

"Well, the Mustangs were arrogant. They continued to run up the score. It must have been thirty or forty runs by then, but it didn't matter. And the woman in the stands started to frown. The way the story goes, as the woman's face darkened, so did the sky. A drizzle of raindrops began to fall, and a bolt of lightning streaked the sky. The game was finally called on account of rain, and the Mustangs fled to their team bus still shrieking with laughter."

Mr. Hawes stopped, took a deep breath, and shrugged. "Who knows if it's true? But what I heard was that it was the last time the Mustangs won a game. The rumor goes that she put a hex on the team for being mean to her grandson."

"Wow," was all Isaac could say.

"Is she still around?" Todd managed to ask.

Mr. Hawes shrugged. "Witch or not, that lady is probably long gone. She'd have to be over a hundred by now. I'm not sure the other school is even there anymore. All those small towns got absorbed into Middleton over the years." He grinned at Todd and Isaac. "Well, that's the story. You boys would be amazed the kind of superstitions even adult pro athletes can hold. I can barely blame teenagers for believing in a curse!"

9

"We're finally getting somewhere," Isaac said as they left Mr. Hawes's house.

"Not a lot to go on, though," Todd said. "A rumor from who knows how many years ago. We don't know a name or even a place."

"But it's *something*," Isaac said, feeling a surge of hope. "We got somewhere despite the curse. That means it can be fought, as long as we know the right questions to ask."

"Yeah!" Todd slapped hands with him. "So what do we do now?"

"I don't know," Isaac admitted. They would have to find a list of schools in the league from 1957 or earlier, and he didn't

know where to begin. When he got home he
scoured the school district website, but there
was no history section. He could call around,
but even if somebody actually knew the
answer, the curse would tie up his tongue if he
tried to ask.

***

Isaac felt the curse settle into his bones a
couple of nights later, pulling him again to
West Side Park. He waited until he was sure
his parents were asleep and left the house
quietly. The sky was heavy and Isaac was sure
it would rain. But he knew from Jaxon that
these night practices were never rained out.
They would have to go on with it even if an
earthquake shook the town and West Side Park
crumbled away.

Why West Side Park? he thought as he
pedaled. Todd said it didn't even exist back
when the curse started. He'd said the original
players must have been standing around in a
cow pasture. Did he know that for a fact, or
was he just cracking a joke?

Maybe the answer to all of this is in the park's history, he thought. He wanted to turn the bike around and pedal home, to research it immediately. But he couldn't do it now. The curse had its hold on him and wouldn't let him go.

***

He practically sleepwalked through the next morning, thinking only about the game coming that afternoon.

Todd joined him at lunch.

"Ready for today's game?" Isaac asked. They were going to play the Creekside High Centurions, the best team in the district.

"Sure," Todd said with a sigh. "Maybe it'll be short and sweet."

They poked at their lunches.

"I hate losing," Isaac said. "Knowing we don't even have a chance."

"Oh, I don't *hate* it," Todd said. "I hate the midnight games and being tired all day, but I don't mind losing. That part is all right."

"What?"

"It's the only thing I can fail at and get away with it. If I mess up in a football game, it's in the newspaper. When I blow it on a test, I hear about it from my parents. But when I strike out, nobody is disappointed in me. Nobody *expects* us to be any good, so it's OK to fail."

That was a strange attitude, but it made sense from Todd's perspective.

"Maybe you should tell people you're scared of bugs," Isaac suggested. "So they know you're not perfect."

"Uh, no," said Todd. "Nobody needs to know about that."

They poked at their food a bit longer. They were both eating the salad, and it wasn't very good that day.

"I'd like it if people expected me to be *good* at something," Isaac said. "Even at baseball, they thought I would quit. I would have, too! The curse wouldn't let me!" He laughed. "The curse has forced me into sticking with it."

"You're turning into a pretty good center fielder, though," Todd said. "If we break this curse, you'd definitely help us win a game or two."

"Thanks, man." Isaac felt a small lump in his throat. He felt like hanging out with Todd wasn't just a shortcut to status anymore, or even a short alliance to beat a curse. They were actually becoming friends.

**

As Isaac squinted into the afternoon sun, trying to see the batter against the glare, he remembered his question from last night.

Why West Side Park?

The park wasn't far from Creekside High School, where they were playing now. The sign in front of the school said "Est. 1972."

What was here before? He wondered.

He was jolted out of his thoughts by a baseball coming his way. He ran back and managed to make the catch. It was finally the third out, after a long inning. The Centurions were already up by four runs, so the curse didn't need him to drop the ball. Isaac tossed it to the umpire and walked slowly back to the dugout. If only this game could end, so he could go home and research it.

Research what? His tired mind tried to recall what he'd just been thinking about. The more he tried to remember, the more it got away from him. It was like trying to remember a dream. Anyway, he didn't have time to think about it. It was his turn to bat.

The Centurions scored fifteen runs in four innings, and the mercy rule was called after the top of the fifth. The two teams lined up and passed each other, slapping hands and saying "Good game, good game." The Centurions couldn't help smirking.

When they got back to the locker room, he saw Korey was already there, peeling off his socks.

"Did you miss the handshake?" Mr. Eglesby asked. He called it *the handshake*, even though really the players just slapped hands.

"Yeah?" Korey looked confused. "I was embarrassed to go out there."

"Don't let it happen again," the coach said sternly.

"It *wasn't* a good game," Korey argued. "We stank."

"It's about sportsmanship," the coach said. "It's required for Mustangs players in every sport to do the handshake."

"So if I don't do it, I'm off the team?" Korey asked, unable to hide the hope in his voice.

The coach grunted and left the room.

"You're not going to get off that easy," Mike told him.

Korey sighed and dropped his socks on the floor.

10

On Saturday morning, after a nice long sleep,
Isaac dumped his backpack out on his desk.
Between baseball and the curse, he'd fallen
behind on homework. He had three sets of
algebra problems to complete, an essay on
the Roman Empire, and a play to read called
Our Town.

The title reminded him of his questions
about his own town. Middleton had grown a
lot in the last thirty or forty years. His dad
talked about it sometimes—how it used to be
a peaceful little town and now it was more like
a big city. It was a center for the tech industry
and had boomed. It had sprawled to the west,

taking over what used to be farmland. Isaac found some info on West Side Park on the city's website, but there was nothing about what was on that spot before. Just info about park features, hours, and rules.

He pushed his work aside and left the house. Maybe Mr. Hawes would have the answer. But when he got to Mr. Hawes's house, it was empty and quiet.

"Are you looking for Bert?" the woman next door asked as he turned around to leave. She was wearing a big floppy straw hat and holding shears, having paused in the middle of trimming her hedges.

"Yeah? Is he all right?"

"I think he will be, but he's gone to the hospital," she said seriously. "Something to do with his blood pressure. Or maybe his blood sugar?" She looked thoughtful. "Well, he'll be there for a few days. Sorry to break it to you."

"Thanks."

"He's no spring chicken, you know."

"I know." The woman couldn't have been much younger than Mr. Hawes. "He used to teach at my high school," Isaac explained. "I've been, uh, researching the history of the school and he's been a big help. Have you always lived in Middleton?"

"No, sorry. I'm afraid I'm a transplant. I can't help you with your research."

"No problem. Just thought I'd ask."

"Bert is at the Middleton Hospital, if you want to see him."

"Thanks."

Isaac walked back home, wondering if the curse had gotten to Mr. Hawes. *She said it wasn't serious, but maybe . . . maybe it needed him to be out of the picture for a while, so we couldn't ask any more questions?* It seemed far-fetched, but so were baseball curses and witches, and those had proven to be very real.

***

Back at home, he worked through what felt like a hundred math problems and read the play. He reached for the next homework assignment. His eyes fell on the folder from the coaches' office. "Baseball 1958." That was fourteen years before

Creekside High was built. Maybe the Mustangs had played whatever school used to be there.

He slid the cards out and started going through them, looking at the school names. Most were familiar to him. Emerson. Fairview. Oakville. Jefferson. *Watertown*.

That wasn't a name he recognized. He looked at the card. There was no final score penciled at the top, so maybe things had gotten so bad the coach stopped trying?

But no. He looked at the scorecard and saw it was the Mustangs who'd been scoring a lot of runs. He felt giddy with excitement. He'd looked from the top of the stack, thinking they were the beginning of the season, and seen huge losses for the Mustangs. But the cards were stacked backward, with the final games on top. The coach back then must have just slid each one into the folder after each game.

So every game that happened after this one was a loss for the Mustangs. But this one, from May 8, 1958, was different. The Mustangs hadn't actually *won*, but they didn't *lose*.

And the one before that was a win. Nine runs to four against Jefferson.

The unfinished game was when the curse started. And the name of the school was right there. *Watertown*. Isaac could even make out the tiny penciled-in name of the fifth and final pitcher for Watertown: J. Juszczak.

He needed to share this with someone. He snapped a photo with his phone to send to Todd, but Todd wouldn't know what it meant. It was more than Isaac wanted to type out on his phone.

Dude, I have something to show you, he texted. *Where do you live?*

1144 Maple. White house on a hill.

Be right there.

Isaac slipped the card back into the folder, pushed the folder into his backpack, and ran outside to his bicycle. He started pedaling for Todd's house, realizing only after he'd gone a few blocks that he was going the wrong way. Maple was north, not south. He'd lived in this neighborhood his whole life. How could he make a mistake like that?

But after turning the bike around and heading the other way for a while, he didn't recognize the street names. King? Palisade? Vermont? Where *was* he? He stopped and regarded a row of new houses that all looked the same, with stone facades and peaked roofs. He reached for his phone to pull up a map and realized he'd left it on his desk at home. He'd left in such a hurry.

He rolled his bike toward a street sign, which told him he was at the intersection of King Street and 13th Avenue. He scratched his head. Neither was familiar. But he couldn't have traveled that far from home in such a short time.

He looked up and saw a shimmering yellow cloud heading quickly toward him. It was buzzing. *A horde of wasps*, he realized. They were too angry to be bees. Had he run over their nest?

No time to try to remember if he had. He kicked off and pedaled madly away from the wasps, no longer caring where he was going. The cloud followed, nearly reaching him at times—close enough that he felt a tickle on the back of his neck before he found a new burst of speed, and surged ahead. The droning hum filled his ears, making his head hurt. He imagined running out of steam, being overtaken and stabbed and stung until he was covered with sores.

"Somebody . . . help . . ." He gasped, driving the pedals with tired legs. His voice barely rose above a whisper. Nobody saw him—every street seemed to be barren.

This is how it ends, he thought, but kept on pedaling.

After a half hour of racing through the streets, the wasps finally disappeared. It took him another hour to find his way home.

"Where were you?" his mother asked the moment he walked in.

"Um . . ." He didn't know how to explain what had just happened. "I just went for a ride to blow off steam. I've been doing homework all day. I needed a break."

"I know," she said. "You've been working really hard. It's just that your dinner is getting cold." She steered him into the dining room.

When he finally got up to his room, he saw a text from Todd on his phone.

What happened to you?

I got lost, Isaac typed back, *and chased by wasps.* He might as well tell the whole truth, even if Todd would laugh at him for getting lost in his own neighborhood.

The curse got you, Todd wrote back. *What were you going to show me?*

Isaac had to think hard to remember. *A scorecard*, he wrote. *I found one for the game where we got cursed.*

He wanted to say more but couldn't remember the name of the town, let alone the pitcher's name. The scorecard was still in his backpack, but where was that? He carried his phone downstairs, checking the dining room and then the garage, where he'd parked his bike. It was nowhere to be found. He must have lost it.

The curse got my backpack too, he texted to Todd. *And my memories.*

11

Clouds gathered late Wednesday evening. Isaac hoped the rain would wait, and when it did start to rain, he hoped it would finish before it got dark. It was still coming down hard when he left the house and rode to the park, splashing through puddles and getting soaked. He remembered playing in the rain, but the memories were as fuzzy and vague as old photographs.

He woke up the next morning in dry pajamas, a pile of damp clothes on the floor. He'd managed to take off the wet clothes, but his head felt heavy, and he was sore from head to foot. He'd caught a cold.

Mr. Eglesby looked upset and distracted on the bus ride to the game. He kept running his hand through his hair and muttering to himself.

"What's with him?" one of the players asked. Isaac was half-asleep in one of the rear seats. His head was stuffy, and his chest hurt. Playing today was going to be a nightmare.

"The rain was so hard last night, it flooded his office," Mike explained. "A bunch of stuff got ruined."

Isaac jolted awake. "What was ruined?"

"Nothing important. Just some old files and stuff. But from the way Coach is acting, he might have kept his comic book collection in those filing cabinets." Mike laughed, but Todd shot Isaac a concerned look.

The game was against the Jefferson High Jaguars. The Jaguars hadn't won a game this season either.

"This is our big chance!" Mr. Eglesby said before the game. He had stopped thinking about the damage to the office and was getting excited about the game. "I don't like to kick a man when he's down, but they'll do it to us, so let's get out there and get us a win!"

But the Mustangs were all sniffling and sneezing. A junior laid down on the bench and groaned.

"Wake me up when it's my turn to bat," he said.

"Ryan, you're the starting pitcher," said Mike.

"Oh, yeah."

Todd and Mike helped him up and out of the locker room.

Nobody scored for the first three innings, but the Mustangs scored a run in the top of the fourth, after Mike reached first on an error, got to second on a stolen base, reached third a bunt, and came home on a sacrifice fly ball.

"It's our first lead all season," the coach said, rubbing his jaw in disbelief. "It might be the first lead in . . . I don't know how long." He looked happier than Isaac had ever seen him. Even the ruined office was forgotten. "This could be my first win as coach!"

Isaac used his phone to snap a photo of the scoreboard. Visitors 1, Jaguars 0. If they never again had a lead, at least he had this to look at.

But then the Jaguars loaded the bases in the bottom of the inning. The puniest Jaguar player came to the plate and took one feeble swing at Ryan's fastball. The ball seemed to be lifted by a sudden strong wind, flying high into the outfield.

Isaac ran after it but could only watch as the ball skipped across the top of the fence and out of the ballpark. It was a grand slam home run. The Mustangs were now behind, four to one. The fans in the stands cheered and stomped.

The curse wins again, Isaac thought.

***

It seemed like the curse was closing in. The horde of wasps that had chased him across town, the rainstorm, the flood in the coaches' office, the gust of wind that had carried that baseball out of the park.

What will happen if we keep trying to break the curse? Isaac wondered as they rode home. *What will it do to us?*

"Coach looks bad," Todd whispered, giving him a nudge. Mr. Eglesby was sitting in the seat in front, his head slumped on his chest.

"He thought we had a chance," Isaac whispered back. "We even had a lead for a few minutes." He remembered the photo he'd taken. He took out his phone to find it. Then he noticed the second-to-last thumbnail in the gallery.

"Hey!" he said. "I took a photo of that scorecard! I was going to send it and didn't because I wanted to show you the card, then I forgot about it because of the wasps and everything." He tapped on the thumbnail, then enlarged the photo. "They played . . . Watertown," he said, squinting at the screen.

"Never heard of it," said Todd.

"It was wiped off the map before we were born." Isaac slid the picture up to see the play-by-play. "The last pitcher's name was J. Jus-z-c-zak," he tried, stumbling over the consonants.

"Jay ja–what?" Todd squinted at him.

"Jus-z-c-zak," Isaac tried again, then spelled it out.

The coach suddenly twisted around in his seat.

"You shock," he said.

"I shock?" Isaac asked, confused.

"That name," the coach said. "It's pronounced *You-shock*."

"How do you know?"

"Because I know Mr. Juszczak. And so do you, sort of. Johan Juszczak comes to all of our home games. He sits behind the dugout. His favorite word is *pathetic*."

"That old heckler!" Todd said.

Isaac's jaw dropped. The man must be in his seventies now, which meant he'd been a teenager sixty years ago. His first initial and last name were the same as that boy who pitched against the Mustangs in the last game they didn't lose. And Mr. "You-shock" sure seemed to hate the Mustangs. It could be a coincidence, but all the pieces fit.

But who carries a grudge that long? he wondered.

12

The Mustangs had another game on Tuesday, which meant another ghastly night game on Monday. Isaac dragged himself to West Side Park even though he was still sick from Wednesday night's ritual in the rain. Even as he was cycling over, he felt a few raindrops. There was another storm coming. Which meant his cold would get worse, maybe even turn into pneumonia.

He'd seen the other Mustangs coughing and sneezing, and knew he didn't have it the worst. But the curse would draw them here, however sick they were.

This weather isn't bad luck, he thought. *It's a warning.*

The clouds seemed especially low over the field at West Side Park. He entered the dreamlike trance and went through the motions of a game, through showers that came and went, and rode home against an icy wind.

Go ahead, he thought. *Do your worst, curse. I'm not going to stop trying.*

***

The game was at home against the Fairview High Aces. As Isaac ran out to center he turned and saw Mr. Juszczak in his usual place in the stands. Before he seemed like a cranky old man, but now Isaac saw him as a dark wizard. One who could summon dark clouds and swarms of wasps, sudden gusts of winds and flash floods.

What could he do about it? He had tracked down the man who might be at the center of the curse, but didn't know what to do next.

The Aces scored four runs in the top of the first inning. As the Mustangs walked back to the dugout, Isaac glanced again at Mr. Juszczak above the dugout. He was scowling at them, as always.

"Pathetic!" he called down to them.

Isaac waved. What else could he do?

"We need to talk to Mr. J," he whispered to Todd in the middle of the seventh inning. The Mustangs were now losing eight runs to none.

Todd nodded once. "OK. But I don't think he wants to talk to us."

"I know, but we have to try. You batted last inning, so I probably won't get a chance this time. See if you can get up there and talk to him."

"All right." Todd stood up. "I've got to, uh, blow my nose," he told the coach, and hurried into the locker room.

The leadoff hitter got on base. That meant Isaac was in the hole, which meant standing at the dugout door. He'd have a chance to bat unless there was a double play.

The next batter struck out, and Isaac went on deck. He took practice swings while the next batter hit a deep fly ball. It was caught for the second out. The runner on first scampered to second. Isaac was the last hope for the Mustangs.

And the last hope for Todd, who was trying to get to Mr. Juszczak. He glanced into the stands and saw that a lot of the home crowd was already up and heading for the exits. He saw Todd heading up the steps, trying to get around the fans who were leaving.

Mr. J was standing, but looking out at the infield, clutching the brass rail. He wouldn't leave until it was over.

I need to keep the game from ending, Isaac thought.

"You're at the plate!" the umpire barked.

He walked as slowly as possible to the plate. He tightened his laces, adjusted his batting gloves.

"Quit stalling," said the umpire.

Isaac sighed and took his stance in the batter's box. The pitcher went in the stretch and flung the ball. Isaac stepped back.

"Stee-rike!" the umpire said.

He swung at the next pitch and hit the ball foul. He fouled off another pitch, and another. It was all he could do to get his metal bat out in time to graze the ball.

On the fifth pitch, the bat hit the ball funny but the ball skipped through the infield, past the shortstop. Isaac looked on in surprise, until he heard the coach hollering at him to run.

He dropped the bat and hurried to first. The runner on second ran all the way home. It wasn't a lead, but Isaac had batted in a run. His first RBI! The players in the dugout all cheered.

This is what it's supposed to feel like, Isaac thought, remembering his reasons for joining the team. He forgot for a moment about the curse.

The next batter struck out, stranding Isaac at first and ending the game. Todd made it back to the field in the nick of time to do the handshake. The two teams walked by the other team, slapping hands and saying "Good game," as they always did. A few of the Aces said "Good hit" to Isaac, and seemed to mean it.

"What happened to Mr. J?" he asked Todd on the way to the locker room.

"He got away," Todd said. "But I saw where he went. He didn't head for the parking lot. He went the other way, which means he walked. And I know which way he lives."

"What can we do? Go door to door looking for him?"

"Do you have a better idea?" Todd asked.

"No," he admitted.

They retrieved their street clothes from the locker room and hurried out without changing. Todd pointed out the direction Mr. J had walked. They walked briskly.

"He's probably home by now," Isaac said.

"You never know," said Todd. "He's kind of slow. I'll take that street, you take this one. Send me a text if you see him."

Isaac nodded and started jogging, wondering how many blocks to go before he gave up. He went four or five blocks, checking the side streets. On the sixth block, he saw a man with slumped shoulders keying open a door.

"Mr. Juszczak!" he shouted, remembering the way the coach had pronounced it. The man whirled around and looked at him with in surprise.

"What do *you* want?"

"I just want to talk," Isaac said.

"About what?" Mr. Juszczak asked.

"About our team," Isaac said. "And why you come to every game and yell at us."

"I come to games because I'm bored and I say hard things because they're true," Mr. Juszczak said sharply.

"I think there's more than that," Isaac said.

Mr. Juszczak set his jaw and squinted at Isaac. Isaac was sure he'd pretend to know nothing. Maybe even threaten to call the police. Instead, he got a weary look on his face.

"Can we talk about it inside?" he asked. "I'm tired."

"Of course."

The old man pushed the door open and led him inside.

Isaac was startled by the old-fashioned appearance of the place. The dining room table was Formica and chrome. The chairs were covered in candy cane–striped vinyl. The TV was a box with a tiny, rounded screen. Isaac realized now that even Mr. J's clothes were of a different era.

Mr. J sat down heavily in a recliner in front of the TV. "Have a seat," he said, waving at the dining room. Isaac took one of the chairs from the table and carried it a few feet, finding it much heavier than he had expected. He sat down.

"So, talk," Mr. J said.

"Well . . ." Isaac wondered if the curse would tie up his tongue. "We have a long losing streak," he started. "Going back a few seasons."

"A few dozen seasons," Mr. Juszczak corrected him.

"Exactly. The truth is we're . . . cursed." He managed to spit the word out. Maybe it was possible because Mr. Juszczak knew all about it. With a rush of excitement that he was finally able to talk to someone about the curse, he told the man everything he and Todd had learned. About the game long ago, where the young pitcher had taken the mound, and the grandmother who had stood up and cursed the team. He then told him how he had learned the school's name, Watertown, and found an old scorecard with that pitcher's name.

"*Your* name," Isaac said at last.

"And you really think it's a curse?" Mr. Juszczak said. "Not just that your team stinks?"

"Well, yes, because there's more." Isaac swallowed hard and told him the rest. About the late-night games, the peculiar incidents during games, the silverfish and the wasps.

Mr. Juszczak seemed to fold. Isaac had called his bluff—he did know about the curse.

"My grandmother wasn't a witch," he said at last.

"But it was really you who pitched?"

"That was me," the old man said. "But it wasn't my granny who hexed you. It was me."

Isaac blinked.

"*You* jinxed us? You were just a kid. How did you know witchcraft?"

"I ordered a book of curses from the back of a horror comic book," Mr. Juszczak explained. "They used to have a full page of ads for pranks and oddities."

"I've seen those." Isaac had some old comics at home. "X-ray specs? Little sea people?"

"Exactly. But I always wanted the weird books. *Ghost Hunting. Fortune Telling. How to Read Minds.* I didn't believe any of it, but liked to make believe. It made life interesting." Mr. J clicked his tongue. "This one was called *One Hundred Hexes.* It promised I could prank my friends and get revenge on my enemies. There was one hex that plagued your enemy with bad luck. I was jealous of the Mustangs because they were good. And they were such poor sports. So arrogant! I memorized that hex and used it while I was on the mound."

"What about your grandmother? She stood up and glared at the Mustangs. . . . Or did that not really happen?"

"It did. She was probably trying to help me. She was a good woman. The worst thing about all of this is people blamed her." He sighed. "I wish you boys would win so I could be done with it."

13

Isaac blinked again.

"You *want* us to win?"

"A curse takes its toll on both sides," Mr. Juszczak said. "I've been trying to get out of it myself. It lures me to every home game. I haven't missed one in over fifty years."

Isaac imagined the same forces that pulled them to midnight practice pulling him to game after game, year after year.

"Do you think you can break this curse?" Mr. Juszczak leaned in.

"I do," said Isaac. "But I don't know how. We were hoping . . . well, we were hoping *you* would know how."

There was a banging on the door. Mr. Juszczak sat up, startled.

"Who's that?"

"Hello?" A voice came through the door.

"It's my friend." Isaac realized he'd forgotten to send a text to Todd. "Is it all right to let him in?"

"Sure." Mr. Juszczak covered his eyes again. Isaac went to the door and cracked it open, holding a finger to his lips so Todd would be quiet.

"You were supposed to text me," Todd said in a low whisper.

"I forgot," Isaac whispered back. "How did you find us?"

"His name is on the mailbox."

"Oh." Isaac laughed. If he was a dark wizard, Mr. Juszczak wasn't very good at hiding. The two of them crept back to the living room. Todd saw the man slumped in his chair, eyes half closed.

"Is he OK?"

"I think so," said Isaac. "It was him who made the hex, not his grandmother," he explained. "He wants to end it too, but doesn't know how."

Mr. Juszczak opened his eyes.

"I do know how," he said. "You have to win a game. That's all. If you do, I'll finally be free of it."

"Wait," said Todd. "If you want us to win, why do you heckle us?"

"Because I'm frustrated," Mr. Juszczak said. "Even after all these years, I always get my hopes up that maybe today will be different. I believe you boys will pull it together and beat the curse and I'll be free at last. But you never do." He sighed.

"Easier said than done," Todd muttered.

"I have an idea," said Isaac.

***

Their next game was on Thursday, so they had a practice the following night. It was a warm night, dry and clear. Isaac rode out on his bike, as usual, and waited at the picnic tables for the others. The players came, one by one. They had the same doomed looks they always did, not knowing that tonight might be the last time they had to do this.

Jaxon arrived in his car, and for a moment Isaac thought Mr. Juszczak hadn't come. But then he saw him in the back seat. He'd ridden in the back as if Jaxon was a cab driver. He clambered out and looked around in disbelief at the park, at the expensive suburban houses beyond the enormous lawn and rows of trees.

"My stars," he said. "To think this used to be bleak little Watertown."

"Come on," said Isaac. "Let's play." He led Mr. Juszczak to the mound.

"All you need is three outs," he said. He ran out to center field.

As he peered through the darkness he saw not an old man, but a scared boy, maybe only thirteen years old. The boy produced a ghostly ball from nowhere and pitched. The ghostly batter at the plate swung, connecting with the ball, sending it the outfield.

Isaac finally understood. They were no longer the Mustangs. They were the Watertown Warriors, the hapless small-town

96

boys being crushed by the big-city team. *He wanted them to know how it feels*, he realized. *Well, they sure did . . . for the next sixty years.*

Johan Juszczak hurled a ball at the batter, and gave up another hit.

Mike walked out from the plate to the mound. He patted the boy—the old man—both seemed to exist at once. He said a few things, patted Johan on the back again, and went back behind the plate. Talking him down, as any catcher does to a jittery pitcher.

As the night wore on, Johan made outs. He struck out one of the ghostly batters, then got another to send a slow roller back to the mound. Mr. Juszczak leaped on the ball and threw it with all his might to first base. It landed short, but the first baseman scooped it up in time for the out.

And at last, an hour after that, as the first gleam of sunlight peered over the houses, a batter sent a deep fly ball to straight down center. Isaac turned and chased it, running on his toes. He leaped and caught the chain link with his toes, scrambling to reach out and snare the ball before it cleared the fence. He brought it down and wheeled around, pulling the ball out to show he had made the out. All at once the ball disintegrated in his hand, the opponents disappeared in a fizzle of mist, and the air seemed to clear. Sunlight burst over the rooftops and shone on the field. The third out was recorded and the game was official. The inning was finally over.

14

That afternoon the Mustangs had another game—a home game against the Creekside High Centurions. The Centurions were still undefeated, and took the field looking very sure of themselves. The Mustangs could not have looked worse. Not one of them had slept. They looked limp and pale. Some of them were still shaking off bad colds.

"It's hopeless," Mr. Eglesby said miserably. "Why can't they invoke a mercy rule before the game even begins?"

"Oh, I think we have a chance," Todd told him. "We're way overdue. One of these days a game has to break our way."

"Ha!" the coach said, shaking his head.

"You can do it!" a voice rang out over the dugout. Isaac stepped out and saw Mr. Juszczak, looking as tired as Isaac felt, but smiling and holding a thumb's-up sign.

"Go Mustangs!" shouted another voice. It was Mr. Hawes, out of the hospital, wearing Mustangs yellow and beaming.

Mr. Eglesby came out and stared in disbelief at Mr. Hawes. "I've never seen you at a game before!"

"I hate to see them lose," Mr. Hawes said, "But Johan tells me today might be different."

"Don't get your hopes too high," Coach said.

Isaac laughed, but felt a burst of energy as he ran out to center field. He really thought the Mustangs might win today.

ABOUT THE AUTHOR

Israel Keats was born and raised in North Dakota and now lives in Minneapolis. He is fond of dogs and national parks.

LEAGUE OF THE PARANORMAL

THE GHOST RUNNER

THE PARANORMAL PLAYBOOK

THE ROOKIE TRAP

THE TEAM CURSE

THERE'S MORE THAN JUST TEAM
SUPERSTITION AT PLAY HERE.

Check out all
the •GRIDIRON• Books

GRIDIRON
THE CLUTCH
PAUL HOBLIN

GRIDIRON
THE EXTRA POINT
CHRIS KREIE

GRIDIRON
FALSE START
PAUL HOBLIN

GRIDIRON
THE LATE HIT
K. R. COLEMAN

GRIDIRON
SHOWDOWN
K. R. COLEMAN

GRIDIRON
SIGNING DAY
K. R. COLEMAN